THE MIDNIGHT BARBER

PARHAM WILLIAMS

The Midnight Barber

Copyright © 2019 by Parham Williams

The Midnight Barber is a work of fiction. All incidents, dialogue, and characters, with the exception of well-known historical figures, are products of the author's imagination and not to be construed as real. Where real-life historical persons appear, the situations, incidents, and dialogues concerning those persons are entirely fictional and are not intended to depict actual events or to change the entirely fictional nature of the work. In all other respects, any resemblance to persons living or dead is entirely coincidental.

ISBN 978-1-7335272-3-1

CHAPTER ONE

IF YOU READ MY STORY about the pickle vat murders, you know I had a lot of excitement last summer. Honestly, I never thought I would be that close to death ever again – and live to tell about it. But this summer turned out to be even more exciting – and even more dangerous. Here's what happened.

MORE THINGS ARE GOING on in Moss Point this summer than you can shake a stick at. The most exciting thing, of course, is the war. That's all the grown-ups talk about. And while I don't read the newspaper – except the funnies, of course – I hear all about the war from the newsreels and Daddy's radio. Mother is the only one who doesn't like to talk about it, and that's because my brother Dick, who is six years older than me, can't wait until he's seventeen so he can join the Marines.

Moss Point is different from the rest of Mississippi, Daddy says, because we have the big Ingalls shipyard here – or at least next door in Pascagoula. Thousands of people have poured into town to work at Ingalls, and they have a hard time finding a place to live. Daddy fixed up the "Little House" in our backyard – it used to be the law office of Mr. Charley Wood, the man who built our house many years ago – and rented it to a man who is a welder. I almost never see him because he works the night shift and sleeps all day.

The new shipyard workers have brought a lot of kids with them, and my fifth grade class this fall will double in size, so Mother tells me. That's fine with me. I look forward to meeting them. Maybe there'll be some cute boys!

THE OTHER THING THAT everybody talks about is the "crime wave" – the biggest and scariest thing ever to happen in Moss Point. You better be glad you don't live here because a lot of the men are carrying pistols and the whole town is scared half to death, and that includes kids and grown-ups alike.

You see, there's this criminal who creeps around at night, slips into people's houses, and cuts big hanks of hair off women while they are sleeping. The *Pascagoula Chronicle* calls him the "Midnight Barber," and the police are going crazy trying to catch him.

Mother and her friends are afraid to go out of the house at night, and even more afraid to go to bed. The hardware stores have sold out of Yale locks and guns and bullets and the man at VanCleave who raises guard dogs has sold every last one of them.

Mother is the nervous type and is really worried about the burglar. We live in a rambling old antebellum house that has high ceilings and windows that go all the way down to the floor. It is beautiful but definitely not burglarproof. The doors and windows don't fit real tight and on a windy night the whole house rattles and shakes like an ice cream freezer. It can get scary.

Fortunately, Mother's friend Ruby Nelson sent her handyman over who put big Yale locks on our front door and back door and side door. He didn't have enough locks for the windows but he tested all of them and told Mother,

"They'll hold, Miz Franklin."

I hope so.

Actually, I felt pretty safe until Daddy loaded his shotgun and stuck it under his side of the bed. I just hope he doesn't shoot Mother or Dick or me – especially me.

CHAPTER TWO

JOYCE, EDNA AND PEGGY, my very, very best friends, spend a lot of time at my house during the summer. Our house is up high off the ground and we can walk around under most of it without bumping our heads. It's the perfect place to play. So, as soon as school was out, I put the girls to work helping me build a whole town out of scraps of lumber and some old benches and things. Pretty soon we had a post office, a bank, two stores and a doctor's office. Joyce is the postmistress and Edna and Peggy take turns running the stores and the bank.

I am the doctor.

That's because I have a whole lot of doctor tools. You see, Daddy is the County Agent and has to vaccinate calves and pigs and horses as part of his job. He leaves old syringes and things lying around under the house and I find them and shine them up. Unfortunately, he keeps the medicines locked up so I have to use stuff like water and turpentine to vaccinate my patients.

In case you're wondering, there is no shortage of patients. Most of them are lizards though occasionally a large worm needs a vaccination. Peggy and I are the best lizard-catchers and Joyce sometimes is the nurse and helps hold the patient while I stick the needle in. Edna doesn't like to do any of this so she has to play in her store while we attend to the patients. Unfortunately, my patients always die pretty soon after I vaccinate them.

WE BURY MY DEAD patients in Daddy's flowerbed by the back steps. It's important they have a dignified burial, so we carefully wrap them in toilet paper and bury them at least six inches deep. Then, either Edna or I read one of the short Bible verses that are on every page of Mother's old *Upper Room* devotional books she's thrown away.

One afternoon Joyce was patting smooth the last grave when she asked, "Are y'all scared of the Barber?"

We giggled. But when we thought about it, the giggles faded away.

"I am," Edna said. "I wish they'd catch him before he hurts somebody."

"Well, I'm not," Peggy said. "My hair is so short he wouldn't find anything to cut!"

We giggled again, but not for long.

"I don't think he fools with kids," Joyce said, "but my mother is scared to death. I sure wish they'd catch him."

I didn't say anything, but I did a lot of thinking about what I would do if the Barber came in my bedroom.

CHAPTER THREE

EVERY SATURDAY MORNING we have a parade. Not one we march in, but one we watch. Right on the dot of nine o'clock, Dick hollers,

"Get ready! Here they come!"

Joyce, Edna, Peggy and I are usually under the house playing but, whatever we're doing, we drop everything and run up to the front screen porch. This has the best view of the parade and it's where Dick and his friends are already sprawled on the porch furniture.

"Here they come!" Dick says, whispering this time. "Nobody make a sound. We don't want 'em to know we're watching. That might scare 'em."

Coming along the sidewalk toward us is a "sight for sore eyes," as Papa Dickson would say. And honestly, you wouldn't believe it unless you saw it yourself.

Leading the parade is a youngish man – probably twenty-five or so – followed about ten feet behind by an older lady. This is a little strange, but that's not why we're watching. You see, the man is wearing a black frock coat that goes down to his knees and a tall black hat like the one President Abraham Lincoln wears in a picture I saw in Dick's American History book. Both the coat and the hat are so old they're shiny and the coat sleeves are way too short for the man's long bony arms. Daddy says men haven't worn clothes like that in more than fifty years and the man must have found them in a garbage can somewhere.

To top it off, he walks like he's the king of England – shoulders back and head held high. Every once in a while the top hat slides forward and he eases it back up with the tip of a long black walking stick he carries under his arm. The lady is wearing an old but very clean, very starched dress and her gray hair is combed back and pinned in a tight bun. She walks a little stooped over and always looks tired.

The parade moves silently past us and disappears in the direction of downtown. Dick squints down the sidewalk to make sure they are out of hearing range. Then he stands up and announces:

"Well, you've seen 'em. Dapper Dan and Nettie!"

MOTHER HAD TOLD US the lady's name and that she is a widow who makes a living by taking in washing. Daniel is her son who is "not quite right." In fact, he has trouble making words and usually just nods and smiles.

"He's a hard worker, though," Mother says. "He helps Nettie do the washing and carries the heavy bundles of clothes for her. She's even taught him to iron shirts and pants."

Although we have a colored washerwoman, Mother sometimes takes special things for Nettie to do, things like tablecloths and napkins and dress-up blouses. I remember the first time I got to ride with her to Nettie's house. The dirty things were piled on the back seat so I was sitting up front beside Mother. We drove down Dantzler Street past beautiful big houses sitting way back from the street with lots of shrubs and flowers in the front yards. A few of the houses had tall columns across the front and most of them had broad galleries and porches where you could sit and talk – or just look. I wondered how much money it takes to buy one of those houses.

Pretty soon we turned off on an unpaved road where the houses were a whole lot littler and some were not even painted. But Mother was not looking at the houses; she was enjoying the trees and flowers that grew naturally along both sides of the road.

"Pollye, just look at these giant live oaks and how they arch over the road. Why, it's like we're driving through a green tunnel!"

It *was* sort of like a tunnel, and the Spanish moss trailing down from the limbs made it spooky, even in the daylight. I quickly decided I didn't want to walk along here in the dark.

The further we drove, the worse the smell got. You see, in addition to the huge Ingalls shipyard, Moss Point also has the world's biggest pogy plant. In case you don't what a pogy plant is, I will tell you about it – but not right now because I'm telling about our trip to Nettie's house.

After a couple of minutes, Mother slowed down and turned into a bumpy dirt driveway. I didn't see a house or people, just giant oak trees and a lot of azalea bushes.

"This is Nettie's yard," Mother said. "I'll have to bring you out here in the spring when all the azaleas are in bloom. It's small, but it's just as pretty as Bellingrath Gardens."

The driveway curved around several big oaks and – there it was: a small, unpainted house with a tin roof, a house not much bigger than the Little House in our back yard.

"It's not fancy," Mother said, "but just look how neat and clean everything is. Why, Nettie told me that Daniel rakes and even sweeps the yard around the house!"

Nettie spotted us through the screen door before we got out of the car. She came out wiping her hands on her apron.

"Come in, please mam," she said. "I'll git them things outta the back seat."

THERE WASN'T MUCH FURNITURE in Nettie's front room, just a low davenport covered in shiny fake leather, a couple of old rocking chairs and a pretty little Victorian lamp stand. Her ironing board was set up by the fireplace and two black irons were tilted up on the hearth. It wasn't chilly and I wondered at first why Nettie had a fire going – then I realized that was how she heated the iron she was using to press somebody's pants.

I fidgeted by the door, not sure what to do while Mother explained to Nettie how she wanted a blouse pressed. I was embarrassed when Nettie looked up and saw me, just standing there like a bump on a log.

"Miz Franklin, I bet little Pollye would like to watch Dan'l do some of his bird tricks."

I nodded vigorously. Mother had told me that Daniel had a "way" with birds and small animals, and had tamed some of them and taught them to do various tricks. I wanted to see the show. When Mother nodded agreement, Nettie told me to "step through the kitchen and find a place to set on the back porch." Then she called out,

"Dan'l. Ohhh, Dan'l. Show little Pollye some of your critters and what they can do."

Daniel was sweeping the leaves and trash out of the back yard, using an ordinary broom instead of a rake. When he saw me come out on the porch he grinned and bobbed his head up and down like he was talking, but no sound came out. He shook his head when I started to sit on the porch, and waved for me to come down and sit on a wobbly wood bench that looked like Peggy and I had hammered it together. Then he sat down on the grass beside me, leaned his head back and whistled. Except it wasn't a whistle, it was a bird-call. I couldn't believe what I was hearing. Daniel sounded just like a bird.

For a moment the woods were still, then a bird answered with the exact same call. Then another one called from farther away. Daniel grinned at me and put his finger to his lips. I was to remain still and silent.

He leaned his head back and whistled another kind of call. Almost immediately, the call was answered from a giant camellia bush at the edge of the yard. For the next few minutes Daniel whistled different kinds of birdcalls, one after another. When he stopped to catch his breath, my ears were ringing.

The woods around us were alive with birds, every one singing and whistling as loud as it could.

Daniel winked at me, reached in his shirt pocket and pulled out a piece of pecan that he had shelled. To my amazement, he popped the piece of pecan between his front teeth and – wow! Every bird in the world seemed to be swooping toward us. A Cardinal won the race and perched on Daniel's shoulder. Before I could blink, he plucked the pecan from between Daniel's teeth and hurried away with his prize.

More pecans appeared from the magic shirt pocket – and promptly disappeared. The air around us was filled with fluttering wings, so many I was getting dizzy.

Daniel fished another piece of pecan out of his pocket and twisted around to hand it to me. I didn't know what to do – and must have shown it – because he opened his other palm and pretended to place the pecan in it, then nodded at my clenched fist. I took a deep breath, opened my fist and held my hand out, palm up. Daniel quickly placed the piece of pecan in my palm, looked up at the birds and whistled a couple of tweets.

Wow! This time *I* was the target! Before I could blink, birds – all kinds of birds – were swooping and swirling around me, their wings rustling like a soft breeze. Abruptly, a littlish black and gray bird – Mother later told me it must have been a Junco – perched on one of my fingers. I expected the pecan to disappear instantly, but my little friend was in no hurry. Turning its head from side to side, it carefully inspected me, the dancing black eyes roaming from my tangled hair to the dirt-stained finger on which it perched. I know it sounds crazy, but I suddenly felt embarrassed. I should have washed my hands after playing doctor under the house! And maybe I could have combed my hair a little better!

My little friend, however, apparently concluded that I was acceptable. Quick as a wink, it plucked the pecan from my palm and flew away. For a brief, beautiful moment, I felt I was flying away, too, borne up by a joy that bubbled into laughter. Daniel laughed with me and placed another bit of pecan in my hand.

The next few minutes were a whirlwind of fluttering wings, flashes of vivid color, and vanishing bits of pecan. The magical spell was broken by Mother's call from the porch:

"C'mon, Pollye, it's time to go."

Daniel seemed not to notice as I eased slowly off the bench, careful not to frighten the birds, and hurried to join Mother. Just before we rounded the big azalea bush at the corner of Nettie's house, I hesitated and looked back.

Daniel still sat on the grass, surrounded by birds. A small brown one perched on his shoulder and two others were exploring my bench. As I watched, he lifted his head and whistled a beautiful lingering call. I don't know what it meant, but I know I didn't want to leave.

WE TURNED ONTO DANTZLER Street and Mother spoke for the first time since we got in the car.

"Daniel's an interesting young man." I nodded but said nothing.

"It's a shame he's like he is. Dr. Ely says he'll always be like that." She was quiet for a few minutes, then added,

"Some people are afraid of him because he's so … so different. But I don't believe he'd hurt a soul. He's just so kind and gentle."

"I feel that way, too," I said, "but I wish he could talk. I'd like to ask him how he makes the birds understand him."

In fact, the more I thought about that, the more puzzling it was. How could it be, I wondered, that he can't speak *my* language, but he can speak the language of all the birds?

Chapter Four

OOPS! I ALMOST FORGOT. I promised to tell you about the pogy plant. So here goes.

One of the things I like best about school is the field trips we take. We've been to the paper mill and learned about International Paper and how the Moss Point plant makes cardboard out of pine trees. And we went to the big Dantzler sawmill where they make lumber but it was so noisy we couldn't hear the old guy who gave us the tour.

We all wanted to go to the shipyard to see how they make ships but we couldn't. The man said there was a war on and building ships was "top secret" stuff. I guess he was afraid Peggy, Joyce, Edna and I were German spies.

The best field trip we took, however, was to the pogy plant. Joyce and Edna didn't want to go because it smelled so bad, but the teacher said it was important that we understand how fishermen work and how every fish in the Gulf is valuable.

Before the school bus came to take us to the plant, our teacher gave us what she called a "briefing."

"The pogy," she said, "is one of the most interesting fish we catch. People can't eat them because they are way too oily, but the pogy plant grinds them up and cooks them and extracts the oil."

"What do they do with the oil?" Peggy asked. She's the most curious person in our grade and asks questions about everything.

"You may find this hard to believe, Peggy," the teacher answered, "but it's used in the soap you bathe with and in your mother's cosmetics and in just oodles of things that we use everyday."

Peggy looked like somebody had slapped her. I had to giggle – I knew she was thinking about smearing pogy oil all over herself when she took a bath.

"Now, who can guess what they do with the pogy meat after they cook all the oil out?"

Everybody was quiet. I had no idea what you do with pogy meat.

"It sure would make good cat food." Carl Anderson said. Now, Carl doesn't make very good grades but he always can be counted on to say something practical.

"Carl's smarter than you think," Daddy said once. "All the Andersons are."

The teacher clapped her hands. "Carl, you are absolutely correct. Much of the pogy meat is shipped to a cannery and made into cat food that's sold all over this country. And what's left is used as a protein supplement for hog feed and cattle feed. So you see, that little fish is very important in many ways."

WE FILED DOWN OFF THE school bus and tramped through a big gate into the pogy plant. The man who met us was real nice and led us back to the wooden docks where several big pogy boats were tied up. I liked it back there. The sun sparkled on the water and the strong creosote smell of the wood canceled out the pogy smell. I closed my eyes and breathed as deeply as I could. When everybody was gathered around him, the guide spoke.

"You see those long black nets hanging from the booms?" I opened my eyes and saw he was pointing up at the damp nets draped from two long poles sticking up on each side of the boats.

"Those are purse seines," he explained. "The boats you see here – plus a lot of others – go out in the Gulf early in the morning and search for schools of pogies. There are thousands and thousands of pogy fish in every school. Many bigger fish – tuna, Spanish mackerel, dolphins – follow the schools and feed on the pogy. This attracts flocks of sea gulls that gobble up the scraps left by the big fish – and that's how we find the pogies."

Our guide paused, pointed up at a little seat fastened near the top of what he called "the mast," and explained: "One of the crew – he's called the lookout – sits up there where he has a good view in all directions. When he spots a flock of gulls circling and diving – sometimes they are several miles away – he guides the boat to that spot. When they reach the school of pogies, the crewmen lower the booms and launch the motorboat." He pointed to a very dirty little boat sitting on the deck.

"The crew use the motorboat to drag the seine all the way around the school, herding the pogies closer and closer together. Then they pull a big drawstring – actually it's a cable – at the bottom of the seine, turning it into a giant purse. When the purse is closed tight, the men use that big winch" – he pointed to the greasy black machinery at the base of the mast – "to haul the seine up and dump the fish into the boat's hold. When they have a boatload, they winch in the seine, haul the motorboat on board, and head for home."

The guide squinted down the river. "In fact, here comes a boat now, loaded down with pogies. It'll take him a while to get here, so let's go into the plant and I'll show you how we unload and process the catch."

We followed the man into the plant, being very careful not to get any fish glop on our shoes, and gathered around him. It was noisy and hot inside the building. Machinery was clanking away and steam spurting from a row of gigantic iron kettles made a weird whistling sound.

"As the fish are unloaded from the boat, the men shovel them onto that big conveyor belt over there." The guide pointed to the wide belt moving slowly from the dock toward the back of the plant.

"The machine that's making most of the noise is called the pulverizer," he explained. "The conveyor belt carries the pogies to the top of the pulverizer and dumps them in. There are large revolving knives inside that chop the fish into smaller and smaller pieces until finally it's a mush."

The guide paused. "It's sort of like a giant blender. Anybody here like milk shakes?" Everybody's hand went up.

"Well, instead of blending ice cream, milk and chocolate sauce into a tasty milk shake, this big boy chops up the pogies and blends them into a thick, gooey "fish shake!"

He grinned and most of the boys laughed. Several of the girls, however, looked disgusted. Joyce said, "yuk!"

Still grinning, the guide led us to the back of the plant, explaining as we walked that the "fish shake" goop was pumped from the pulverizer into the giant steam kettles. After several hours of "cooking," the valuable fish oil was drained off and the goop was dried and canned.

Stopping by a big sliding door, he asked if there were any questions. Thank goodness nobody asked one. It was too hot and smelly to hang around and talk. We just wanted to get out and back on the bus.

"OK," the guide smiled, "we enjoyed having you as guests. Please be careful going down the steps."

He rolled open the big door and I saw we were looking out on the parking lot where our school bus waited in the shade of an oak tree. Somebody started clapping. It was our teacher. We all gave a few half-hearted claps and raced for the iron steps leading down to the parking lot.

☙❧

Chapter Five

MOTHER APPARENTLY AGREED with the little Junco, because first thing Saturday morning she loaded me in the car and drove to Ella's Beauty Parlor.

"It's time you had a professional shampoo and trim," she explained.

Two ladies were being worked on when we got there. Miss Ella was rolling up one lady's hair on funny-looking pink rollers. Her assistant, a young lady whose name I never did learn, was washing another customer's hair, rubbing briskly and spattering shampoo bubbles over half the shop.

A third lady was sitting underneath a shiny round thing that looked like a giant beehive made out of tin. The top half of her head was hidden inside the thing and all I could see was her chin – or rather, her chins.

"Come in, Miz Franklin. You and Miss Pollye sit right over yonder and look at the new magazines I got." Miss Ella sounded real proud of her magazines.

"I got *Woman's Home Companion, Ladies Home Journal, Good Housekeeping* and the new issue of *McCall's.*

We sat down and Mother began thumbing through the *McCall's,* one of her favorite magazines. I couldn't take my eyes off the beehive and finally had to whisper to Mother,

"What is that thing on her head?"

"Shhhh," Mother whispered back. "That's a hairdryer. After Miss Ella gives you a shampoo, you sit under that while it dries your hair."

That did not sound like fun. "Do I have to?"

Before Mother could answer, Miss Ella said, "Well, he struck again. The 'Midnight Barber,' the paper calls him. Have you heard about it?"

"Why, no," Mother answered, already worried. "Where did it happen?"

Miss Ella opened her mouth to reply, but a hollow-sounding voice from somewhere in the beehive beat her to it. "Right down the street on Bellview. Not two blocks from the high school!"

Miss Ella looked disgusted, but she was determined to have her say. "That's right. He broke in that old house that's being rented by the young couple, the Smiths."

"The old Hammond house," the beehive said.

Miss Ella frowned at the beehive and said quickly, "Sheila Smith's her name. Husband's in the army."

"At Fort Benning," the beehive said.

Miss Ella stopped rolling hair and glared at the beehive. "Well, I'll tell y'all something nobody else knows." She was determined to have the last word.

The beehive was silent.

"Miz Smith, that's Sheila, telephoned me before I opened the parlor this morning and got an appointment so I could trim and straighten out her hair. She'll be here in" – she glanced at the alarm clock on the counter – "five minutes."

There was a whooshing sound as everybody in the parlor, including the beehive, gasped at the news.

"If it's alright, Miz Franklin, I'll work on Sheila first" Miss Ella said. "I know she wants to get her hair fixed as quick as possible."

"Why, of course," Mother said. "And I don't think we should ask her about it – unless of course she volunteers something.

THEY WERE EARLY. An old black car pulled in and parked in front of the parlor. Three ladies got out, an older lady and two young ones. One of the young ladies had her head wrapped in a bandana of some sort and seemed to lean on the older lady. Miss Ella met them at the door.

"Y'all come on in. Miss Sheila, you set in that first beautician chair and I'll get right to you."

I wanted to see Mrs. Smith's hair – how much of it was cut off – but I knew it would be bad manners to stare at the poor lady. So I forced myself to look straight ahead at a blue-handled hairbrush on the back counter. Actually, this was a good idea because I had a pretty good view of Mrs. Smith out of the corner of my eyes. Looking out the other corner of my eyes I noticed that the beehive lady had slid down in her chair so her eyes were just below the rim of the dryer. She was pretending to look straight ahead, but the eyeball I could see started creeping around – and around – until it almost disappeared in her nose. I sincerely hoped it might get stuck there.

Miss Ella unwrapped the bandana and shook Sheila's hair loose. In spite of myself, I had to swivel my eyes and look straight at her head. Ouch!

The Midnight Barber had whacked out a hank of hair above her right ear, leaving nothing to cover the ear and that side of her head. Although the remaining sprigs of hair were about an inch long, I could see the white scalp shining through.

She was a pretty lady and her remaining hair was auburn-colored and naturally curly. I could tell she'd been crying – her eyes were red and puffy – and she held tightly to the older lady's hand. I decided that must be her mother; maybe the young lady was her sister.

Miss Ella took a step back, hands on hips, and carefully examined each side of Sheila's head.

"That's not so bad, dearie," she said encouragingly. "We're gonna even that up and you'll be pretty as a picture."

She turned and spoke kind of low to the older lady. I couldn't hear all of what she said, but I did hear "hairpiece 'til it grows out" and "just trim it today" and "can get it from Mobile in no time" and "y'all can come back Friday." The lady nodded and they both looked at Sheila who frowned at first, then gave a big sigh and nodded.

Ella pinned an apron around Sheila and started trimming and measuring. I was proud of myself. I didn't peek but three times – well, maybe four times.

Every so often Ella said something softly to Sheila. Other than that, the only sound was the clicking of Ella's scissors. So I'm not exaggerating when I say we almost jumped out of our skins when the beehive suddenly spoke.

"Did he hurt you, honey?"

Ella whirled toward the beehive and started to say something, but Sheila stopped her.

"That's alright. I know y'all are dying to know so I'll just tell you. Then maybe you can leave me be."

The older lady patted Sheila's arm and said, "Now sweetheart, you don't have to … " Sheila interrupted. "No, Mama, I'm gonna tell it." She took a deep breath and started. At first her voice was a little shaky, but then she settled down.

"I was really tired last night and went to bed around nine o'clock. Harold's in the Army, you know, and I was by myself. I made sure the doors were locked – we don't have but a front door and a back door – and tested the windows in our bedroom. The rest of the windows stay locked all the time."

I noticed she wasn't looking at any of us – just staring at the floor.

"I never heard a sound – no clicking of scissors, no footsteps, no nothing. The first thing that woke me up was a pull – a little bitty pull – at my hair on this side." She patted the right side of her head.

"At first I was half dreaming and thought the pulling sensation was part of the dream. Then I felt pieces of hair sort of tickling the side of my face. I still hadn't heard a sound. I opened my right eye … you see, I was laying on my side and my left eye was squashed into the pillow … and I saw this dark … thing right beside the bed. All of a sudden it just come to me … what I was seeing … and I turned cold as ice all over."

"Oh, my," the lady wearing the curlers whispered.

"I didn't know what to do," Sheila continued, "so I pretended to be asleep. That was when he stepped back – I think he must have finished cutting my hair – and the scissors moved through a little beam of light from the street light outside. The reflection – all bright and shiny – made the scissors look just like a razor or a thin knife. That's when I screamed. I couldn't help it. I just screamed – and sat straight up."

"Oh, Lordy!" Ella's voice was hoarse and whispery.

"I know it scared him, 'cause he jumped back and bumped the chifferobe – I remember hearing that pretty little vase you gave me, Mama, rattling back and forth like it was gonna fall off the top where I keep it. You gave it to me for my tenth birthday, and I was so afraid it'd fall off and break."

Sheila shook her head. "You know, it's crazy the things you think of at a time like that."

Ella cleared her throat and asked, "What happened then?"

"Well, we just stared at each other – it seemed like hours but it couldn't have been more than a few seconds. And then," she paused and frowned, "it seemed like he was trying to say something to me, but just couldn't get the words out."

Everybody in the parlor, me included, was staring at Sheila. I don't know about the others, but I was wondering what I would do in that situation.

"The next thing I knew," she continued, "he turned and ran out through the kitchen." She was quiet for a moment and then added,

"When I heard the back door slam, I hopped up and called the police."

Nobody said a word for the longest time. Then the lady wearing the curlers asked, "Did you see his face?"

"No, mam," Sheila answered. "He was wearing a black mask that covered his whole face. He must have been wearing gloves, too, 'cause the police told me they couldn't find a single fingerprint – at least one that didn't belong to Harold or me."

I was hoping there wouldn't be any more questions. I felt so sorry for Sheila. It must have been embarrassing – and painful – to have to talk about such a terrible thing. But I should have known the beehive had another question.

"Did he do anything to you, honey? You know, with his hands or … or anything else?"

Ella almost threw a fit, but Sheila quieted her.

"I know what you're thinking, and probably a lot of other folks, too. So I'll answer you straight out. No, mam! He did not touch any part of my body – with his hands or anything else. Just my hair with the scissors.

NOBODY SAID ANYTHING FOR a while after Sheila and the other two ladies left. Then the voice from the bee-hive spoke.

"He's the one! I know he's the one."

We looked expectantly at the beehive, but the voice was silent. After a moment, Ella asked, "Who're you talking about?"

"I'm talking about that loony son of Nettie's, the woman that takes in washing. Sheila Smith described him perfectly – 'trying to say something but just couldn't get the words out.' That's him! That's him, for sure!"

ೞ⊗ಬ

CHAPTER SIX

I HAD JUST GONE TO BED, so it probably was around nine-thirty, when somebody knocked on our front door. Daddy went to the door – Mother won't answer the door after dark – and asked in a gruff voice, "Who's there?" He must have scared the person because it seemed like ages before a weak little voice answered,

"Is that you, Mr. Franklin?"

I eased out of bed and tiptoed to my door that opens into the living room. I didn't dare open the door, not even a crack. Somebody would spot me for sure and I would be ordered back to bed before I could say "Jack Robinson." But I was determined to hear what they said, so I put my ear to the keyhole and waited.

"Why it's you!" Daddy sounded surprised. "Come on in. I'll get Maud."

"Who is it, Arlis?" I heard Mother's voice back in the hall but couldn't make out Daddy's answer. Mother must have hurried into the living room because her voice was much closer when she spoke again.

"Why, Honey, what's the matter?"

There was silence for a moment so I squatted down and peeked through the keyhole. I couldn't see our visitor's face but I recognized the dress – the same dress she had worn in last Saturday's parade. I could see her hands, too, and they were twisting a damp handkerchief around and around her fingers.

"I didn't know who to turn to, Miz Franklin, but y'all have been so good to us that I thought … I thought … you might … ." Nettie's words ended in a sob that caught in her throat.

The back of Mother's housecoat swished across my view and I knew she was hugging Nettie. In a moment she said,

"It's alright, Nettie. We don't mind your crying. But tell us. What in the world is the matter?"

"Miz Franklin," Nettie could barely get the words out, "they done … they done … arrested Dan'l!"

There was a moment or two when all I heard was Nettie's sobbing. I guess Mother and Daddy were too shocked to say anything. Then Daddy spoke.

"Why did they arrest him, Nettie? What did they say?"

Nettie struggled to answer. "The police … they said … they said … he was this man who's … cuttin' … ladies' hair at night!"

The only sound was Nettie crying. Then Daddy said, "I'm going to call the Sheriff's Office and find out what's going on."

Mother must have led Nettie back to the kitchen because their voices faded away. A terrible feeling came over me, like

I was sick at my stomach. I slid down the door and sat on the floor. I never felt so miserable in my life. How could the police be so wrong? Daniel was the last person in the world who would slip into people's houses and cut ladies' hair.

I could faintly hear Daddy's voice, back in the hall, talking on the telephone. The only words I could make out were, "Monday morning? OK." With that, he hung up. When the ladies came back into the hall, Mother was talking.

"We can't find out any more tonight, Nettie, so Arlis is going to take you home. We'll let you know, as soon as possible, what can be done."

JOYCE AND I WERE PLAYING under the house Monday when Daddy came home to eat dinner. I remembered he was going to talk to the Sheriff sometime that morning, and I wanted to hear what he'd found out about Daniel. Joyce would be in the way so I asked her nicely to go home.

"It's dinner time. You'd better go home or Elizabeth will be mad at you."

Joyce is the one who got mad.

"Well, you *could* be nice enough to invite me to eat dinner with y'all. Then we could play all afternoon." She was wearing her super-pouting face.

"No," I said. "You need to go home!"

That made her madder than ever. I actually could see steam coming out of her ears.

"You can bet I'm going," she hollered, "and I'm never coming back to your stinking house, you ... you ... German spy!"

"German spy" was the worst thing we could think of to call somebody during the war, and it made me really mad. I grabbed up the first thing I could find to throw at her. It turned out to be one of my vaccinated patients – a big lizard that had died yesterday and we hadn't got around to burying. It landed square in the middle of Joyce's face. She let out a screech you could hear in Pascagoula and tore out across our back yard to her grandmother's house next door. Every step of the way she was screaming,

"German spy! German spy! Dirty stinking German spy!"

BY THE TIME I GOT in the kitchen, Mother and Daddy were seated at the little table on the Sun Porch where we mostly eat. I knew if I barged in and sat down with them, Daddy probably wouldn't say much about what he'd found out. So I tiptoed across the kitchen and hid behind the half-open door. Lena turned away from the sink and started to say something to me. Quick as a wink, I put my finger to my lips and then held my hands together like we do when we're praying, silently begging her not to say a word. She took a deep breath and I just knew she was about to say something – but then she heard Daddy begin to tell what he'd learned at the jail. That did it. Lena tiptoed over and stood on the other side of the door. She wanted to hear the news, too.

Daddy was talking. "Let me tell you this quick before Pollye gets here. I drove over to Pascagoula early this morning so I could catch Raymond before he got tied up in something."

Lena and I looked at each other. Both of us knew that Daddy was talking about Mr. Raymond Hardy, the Sheriff of Jackson County.

"Raymond and I've been friends for years and I knew he'd tell me what he could. Seems that the Moss Point police are convinced that Nettie's boy is the hair cutter, but right now they don't have much of anything in the way of real evidence. By the way, Raymond doesn't think much of their investigation, either, said they're all as dumb as a row of fence posts. Said all they've really got is what this last woman – what's her name?"

Mother quickly answered, "Sheila Smith."

"That's right, what Mrs. Smith told the police. She said the masked man seemed to be trying to say something to her, but just couldn't get it out."

"Yes," Mother said. "I heard her say that in the beauty parlor." They were quiet for a moment, then Mother added, "But she didn't seem very sure that's what the man was trying to do. I think she's just guessing."

"Well, anyway," Daddy continued, "Raymond said that if the police don't come up with something more, Sam Anderson is going to ask Judge McCaleb to release Daniel on some kind of bail. Said they can't keep him locked up just on that woman's guessing."

I looked over at Lena and mouthed, "Who is Sam Anderson?"

She mouthed something back that I couldn't interpret, so she tried again.

"Dee-strict At-torn-ey." I got it that time.

"What made me mad, though," Daddy said, "was what the Moss Point police did to Nettie's house. Raymond said they searched that little house from top to bottom, and when they left, it was a mess. Clothes lying on the floor, mattresses cut open, just a mess."

A coffee cup clattered on a saucer and Mother said, her voice as sad as I've ever heard it, "That's horrible. Just awful."

"And you know what they found?" Daddy didn't wait for an answer. "Well, Raymond said the only thing they found and seized as evidence was a little pair of scissors that were in Nettie's sewing box."

I heard Mother sort of groan.

Daddy continued. "Raymond got the scissors out of the safe and showed them to me. Why, you couldn't cut a hank of hair with those little things if you sawed a whole week!"

Chapter Seven

PEGGY CAME OVER AFTER dinner and we played most of the afternoon under the house, straightening a couple of the streets, rearranging the post office, and building a new cafe. Edna was supposed to come over, too, but she never showed up. Joyce was nowhere to be seen.

Peggy and I were drinking a Coca Cola in the new café, pretending it was French wine, when Mother called from the back porch. Her voice sounded stern, which is very unusual for Mother, and I had the sinking feeling I was in trouble. I quickly tried to think of all the things I might have done wrong, but all I could remember was throwing the dead lizard at Joyce. That wasn't so bad, was it?

"Pollye, I need to talk to you. Come up here right now!" Mother's voice was louder this time.

Peggy hopped up and brushed the dust off her sunsuit. "It's gettin' late, Pollye. I gotta go home."

I didn't blame her. In fact, I was wishing I could go with her.

MOTHER LED ME INTO THE Sun Porch – I guess I was too dirty to sit anywhere else – and sat me down on the footstool Daddy puts his feet on when he's reading the paper.

"Elizabeth called a few minutes ago." There was no smile in Mother's voice.

"She said you hit Joyce with a dead lizard."

Uh, oh. I had to think fast. I would never, ever tell a lie to Mother – still, this was an unusual situation.

"Well, you see," I said, "it was kind of an accident."

Mother's eyebrows arched up. "How was it an accident, Pollye?"

"Well, it was dinner time, time for Joyce to go home, and I suggested that both of us should go eat with our parents. I don't know why, but Joyce got mad and called me a bad name, a *really* bad name."

Mother looked interested. "What did she call you?"

"*A German spy!*" I tried to put as much meanness as possible into each word. Mother tried to look serious but the beginnings of a smile tugged at the corner of her mouth.

"That's not a nice thing to say," she said, "but you should not have thrown a dead lizard at her. I'm disappointed in you."

"Well, you see, I really just wanted to scare her, but the lizard was slippery and it just … uh … kind of … uh … missed and … uh … hit her."

"Uh, huh," Mother sounded unconvinced. "Well, here's what you're going to do. March straight to your bathroom, take a quick bath, brush your hair, and put on a clean dress. That blue one you wore to Sunday School will be fine."

I opened my mouth – but quickly closed it. There was no use saying anything else. I was guilty and we both knew it.

"When you are dressed," Mother continued, "we're going to Elizabeth's and you're going to apologize to Joyce."

I had a sinking spell. Apologizing to Joyce was the worst thing that could happen to me. But there was no escape.

GUESS WHO OPENED THE door when Mother rang the bell. You're right: Joyce! She was so clean she sparkled and had on her prettiest Sunday School dress – Elizabeth called it a frock. Her naturally curly blonde hair had been brushed and brushed until it was … well, beautiful.

"Come in, please," Joyce spoke primly. "We're having refreshments in the dining room."

She led us into the spacious room where the table was set for five with crinkly pink doilies and Elizabeth's best silver at each place. Tall white candles, set in silver candelabras, cast a soft glow over the table. I suspected the candle lighter must have been Mary, Joyce's little sister. My suspicion was confirmed when I spotted at least five burnt kitchen matches half hidden under a napkin.

We were barely seated at the table when the kitchen door magically swung toward us and a hand appeared, holding the door half open. I knew it was Elizabeth's hand because I recognized the diamond in her wedding ring, a diamond the size of a Dubble Bubble Gum ball.

Mary marched carefully through the door, her eyes fixed on the plate of coconut cake slices she was carrying. Cautiously, step-by-step, she approached the table, paused, then began a struggling attempt to lift the heavy cake plate to the table top. It was too much. Half way up the plate began to tilt – and tilt – and tilt!

Mother's strong hands came to the rescue! Carefully, she guided the plate onto the table, then gave little Mary a quick hug. Together, they placed slices of cake on each of our plates. As they finished, Elizabeth came bustling in with a half gallon bucket of vanilla ice cream in one hand and a scooper in the other.

"I just know everybody needs a big scoop of ice cream on top of their cake!"

In moments, giant blobs of ice cream had plopped on each piece of cake. I could hardly wait to take a bite. Mary's spoon already was in motion.

"Just a moment, Mary dear," Elizabeth cautioned, "Joyce and Pollye have something to say before we eat."

She was looking straight at Joyce who squirmed, twisted her mouth, and kept her eyes on the ice cream. We leaned forward to hear the mumbled apology.

"We couldn't hear that, Joyce," Elizabeth said with a touch of sternness in her voice.

Joyce took a deep breath, squinched her eyes closed and announced:

"I'm sorry I called you a GERMAN SPY!"

The ball was now in my court. I was determined not to mumble, so I also took a deep breath and said, as calmly as I could:

"And I'm sorry I threw ADOLPH at you!"

There was an awkward silence for a moment. Then Mary, who was staring at me wide-eyed, asked, "The lizard was named Adolph?"

"Yes," I quickly answered. "You see, it had a little black spot under its nose that looked just like Adolph Hitler's moustache. So, we named … ." The rest of my explanation was drowned out by Mary's squeal.

"The lizard was named Adolph!" She howled with laughter. "Adolph! Adolph!" She was laughing so hard she almost choked on the last "Adolph!"

Her laughter was infectious. In a moment we all were laughing, laughing so hard tears were running down our cheeks. Joyce and I reached toward each other at the same time and, for several long minutes, held hands across the table, laughing like crazy people.

When we calmed down a little, Joyce said softly, "You're my best friend."

I swallowed and said, "And you're my best, best friend – ever."

The ice cream and coconut cake were heavenly!

Chapter Eight

A WEEK WENT BY AND the Moss Point police were still "investigating" the case of the Midnight Barber. Despite all their searching and interrogating, however, they had found no more evidence linking Daniel to the hair cutting.

Around ten o'clock that Monday morning, I was sitting with Mother in the Sun Porch, both of us reading. The only sounds were the gentle whirring of the electric fan Lena had placed on the table and soft sloshings from the kitchen where she was washing the breakfast dishes.

Suddenly, the telephone jangled harshly. Mother and I both jumped. She answered and I returned to reading *The Adventures of Huckleberry Finn*. Our fourth grade teacher had said the book was "too difficult" for us and we shouldn't waste time trying to read it. She was wrong. I was enjoying it tremendously.

I put the book down, however, when I heard Mother say, "In this morning's paper? She was quiet for a moment, then asked, "Can you read it to me?" More silence, then Mother said in an irritated voice, "Well, then, I'll read it for myself!" She hung up abruptly.

"Sometimes your Daddy can be the most exasperating man in the world!"

I said nothing – wisely. In a moment, she turned to me.

"Pollye, would you mind stepping out on the front porch and bringing me the morning paper? I forgot to bring it in."

"Yes, mam," I said, squirming out of my chair.

WHEN I HANDED HER THE paper, hot from lying in the morning sun, she unfolded it and smoothed out the front page. Adjusting her glasses, she read for several minutes, then put the paper down in her lap and dabbed her eyes with a Kleenex.

"Thank you, Lord, thank you." Her voice was a soft murmur.

I was quiet as a mouse. I knew she would tell me the news if I were old enough to hear it. If not – well, I would just keep on reading *Huck Finn*. She turned to me, her eyes moist with happiness.

"Pollye, this is the most wonderful news – news I've been praying, praying every day, to hear."

"Yes, mam."

"The judge has released Daniel from jail! Said there was not enough evidence to … ." She glanced down at the paper and read, " … to establish probable cause to believe that the prisoner is guilty."

She dabbed at her eyes again. "I'm going over to Nettie's right after dinner. Maybe I can help her get everything straightened out. You can go with me, if you want to."

"I do! I do!" I was grinning and giggling like a crazy person. I wanted to tell Daniel how happy I was that he was free – that I always knew – just knew in my heart – that he was innocent. Also, I wanted to feed the birds again.

DADDY CAME IN A FEW minutes later and he and Mother immediately went into their bedroom and closed the door. I knew they didn't want me to hear their conversation, so that just made me more determined to hear what they were saying.

They must have known I would try because they were talking softly and, no matter how tightly I pressed my ear to the door, all I could hear was low mumbling. I knelt down to peek through the keyhole and – would you believe it? Something, a Kleenex or something, was stuffed in the keyhole.

I could only shake my head. It's so sad. Parents just don't trust their children anymore.

MOTHER BRAKED TO A STOP while we were some distance from Nettie's front steps and murmured, "Oh, my goodness! How awful!" I had been searching the trees for Daniel's birds and hadn't noticed what upset her. Now I saw it.

Tire tracks, big tire tracks, cut an ugly path across the yard and right through a clump of azalea bushes. The azaleas, which must have been so beautiful a couple of months ago, were now just splintered limbs and scattered leaves.

"Who would have done such a thing?" Mother was speaking to herself, not to me. I didn't try to answer.

Nettie met us on the porch. I could tell she'd been crying, but she managed a lopsided smile. "Oh, Miz Franklin, I 'preciate you coming. It's been a hard day."

Mother put an arm around Nettie's thin shoulders and led her back into the house. She looked back at me and said, "Wait here on the porch, Pollye. I won't be long."

She closed the front door behind them. I edged as close to it as I dared.

"Arlis told me about what happened out here, Nettie. It must have been terrible." Mother was speaking softly, but I could hear almost every word.

"Yes, mam. We was skeered half to death. I was fixin' dinner in the kitchen when I heered the truck. They made a big circle through the yard and throwed some rocks that mostly hit on the roof." She paused for a moment. "'Cept for that one what broke the winder."

For the first time, I noticed the broken windowpane – and the spatters of dried mud on the wall beneath the window.

"But the worsest thing, Miz Franklin, was what they hollered."

"What was that, Nettie?"

"They hollered Dan'l's name and … " she made a choking sound like she was trying to keep from crying, " … and said they was comin' back tonight to git him."

Nobody said anything for a while. The only sound was Nettie's sniffling. Then she sort of half-whispered, "Oh, Miz Franklin, I don't know what to do."

"Well, let me tell you what Arlis said. He said to tell you that he and the Sheriff talked about it, and they both feel Daniel would be a lot safer if he slept at the jail, at least for the rest of this week. One of the deputies will bring him out here every morning in time to have breakfast with you and then pick him up after supper."

"Oh, Miz Franklin, that'll skeer pore Dan'l to death. Please. No! No!"

"Shhhhh," Mother quieted her. "The Sheriff said you can stay with him if you want to."

"You mean I kin stay there all night in the jail with Dan'l?"

"Yes. Both of you will be safe there."

"Oh, Lordy, that'll be our salvation. Thank you, Lord, thank you."

"Well, don't forget to thank the Sheriff, too," Mother reminded her.

"No mam, I won't. Now, if you'll excuse me, I gotta go holler Dan'l up and feed 'im 'fore the deppity gits here."

"Yes, you need to do that," Mother said. "By the way, where is he?"

"I'm pretty sure he's hidin' in a little tree house he built a few years ago. Says he made it just for hisself and the birds."

ℰℐℰ

Chapter Nine

SPENDING EACH NIGHT LOCKED in a jail cell indeed proved to be Daniel's salvation. For on Friday night, while Daniel and Nettie were sleeping safely and securely in the Jackson County Jail, the Midnight Barber struck again.

Mother and I hugged when we heard the news the next morning. "Oh, Pollye, that settles it once and for all," Mother said, her voice trembling with emotion. "Daniel is *not* the Barber! He's *not* guilty!"

Her arms tightened and she held me quietly for a moment. When she spoke again, there was no joy in the words.

"That poor, poor woman."

Her voice faded and she turned her head away. I knew she didn't want me to see the tears. To tell the truth, I felt like crying myself, something I almost never do.

You see, there was something very different about what had happened. The Barber not only cut the victim's hair – he also murdered her.

ONCE AGAIN, LENA AND I stood quietly just outside the Sun Porch door and listened as Daddy told Mother what he had learned.

"Raymond told me the woman – her name, by the way, was Leona Murphy – lived by herself and worked as a secretary at the shipyard. She had pretty red hair and the barber had whacked a hank off one side. Raymond said she must have waked up and fought the man because she had a bunch of stab wounds – defensive wounds, he called them – on her hands and arms. They bled a lot but that's not what killed her."

Nobody said anything for a moment. I heard an ice tea glass click down on the table.

"Well, what killed her, Arlis?"

"Raymond said they wouldn't know for sure until he gets the autopsy report. They're sending the body this afternoon over to Mobile. There's a medical examiner over there the county pays to do our autopsies."

"But do they have to wait on that to know what killed her?" Mother asked.

"Officially, yes," Daddy replied. "But Raymond had Dr. Farnsworth look at the body this morning. According to the doc – just looking at her from the outside and not cutting her open – death was caused by a stab wound to the heart. Said the wound looked to him like it was caused by a pair of sharp pointed scissors."

I looked over at Lena. Her eyes were as round as saucers. Mine probably were, too. In any event, we both jumped half out of our skins when Mother called.

"Lena, please bring the pitcher of ice tea in here. Mr. Franklin's glass is empty."

"Yes'm, it's on the way." Lena scurried off to get the ice tea.

When she came back, we both lingered by the door in case Daddy had any more information. He did. And it was puzzling.

"Raymond said when Dr. Farnsworth was looking at the body, he all of a sudden bent over and sniffed around the nose and mouth. Then he called Raymond to come over. 'Get down close to her face,' Farnsworth told him. 'Do you smell anything?'"

Daddy was quiet again. The ice tea glass clicked on the table and I heard him crunching ice.

"You're bound to break a tooth one of these days," Mother warned as she always did when he chewed ice. Of course, he never paid any attention to her. When the crunching stopped he spoke again.

"Raymond said he caught the faint smell of chloroform. The doc agreed. Said in his opinion, the barber was attempting to chloroform the woman when she woke up and tried to fight him."

I looked over at Lena. This time her mouth was open as wide as her eyes.

I DON'T HAVE TO TELL YOU that life in Moss Point speeded up considerably after that. All kinds of policemen – state, local, even the FBI – came to town. Daddy said the FBI was called in because the shipyard was doing secret government work and the murderer might be targeting shipyard workers. In any event, law enforcement people were swarming everywhere. It was really, really exciting.

One thing happened, though, that was no fun. I was ordered to sleep in Mother and Daddy's bedroom. I quickly found out that it did absolutely no good to complain.

"Don't argue, Pollye," Mother said firmly. "You are going to sleep in our room and that's that! I'll fix a pallet for you beside our bed."

"But I don't want to sleep on a pallet," I wailed.

"Then you can sleep in the bed with us," she responded sharply.

I quickly decided the pallet wouldn't be so bad, after all.

CHAPTER TEN

RUMORS OF ALL KINDS floated back and forth, and new ones were invented every day. One that many people believed involved a burglar who was famous all over Europe for stealing the crown jewels of three different kings, including the king of England. Shortly before the war broke out, the French police caught him and he was locked up for life in a dungeon. When the Germans captured France, they made a deal with the guy. They would take him in a submarine to Pascagoula where he would scare everybody by breaking into houses and cutting ladies' hair. The shipyard workers would be so scared they would quit their jobs and the shipyard would have to close down. Then the Germans would give the man one million dollars in gold and set him free.

That sounded like it might be true to Peggy and me, but Joyce said "no." Her daddy had heard some police guys drinking coffee in the drug store say it was a crazy man who escaped from Whitfield. They knew for a fact that the guy was a skit-something-or-other who had two personalities. During the day he was a normal person who was very polite and a hard worker who went to the Presbyterian Church every Sunday. As soon as the sun went down, however, he changed into a different person who put on black clothes and a black mask and collected women's hair as a fettish (I don't know how to spell it and I don't know what it is, but that's what Joyce's daddy said).

Daddy told Dick and me not to believe any of the rumors, that people were dumb to start them and even dumber to believe them. He was probably right, but Joyce, Edna, Peggy and I had a lot of fun talking about the murder and making up our own stories about the killer. We got together every day and drank Coca Colas in our café under the house and told all the latest rumors we had heard. Some of them were really scary but they were the most fun of all.

Chapter Eleven

A WEEK WENT BY AND nobody got arrested. Mother and Elizabeth were nervous wrecks and Eva, that's Edna's mother, wouldn't leave the house – not even in the daytime. After a few more days the excitement began to die down and was replaced by a sense of dread.

"We know he's out there," I heard Mother say to Elizabeth one afternoon. "And it could be someone we see every day."

"Yes," Elizabeth said. "And we know he's going to strike again – maybe even kill!"

They were quiet for a while, then Mother said, "We can only pray that the victim won't be one of our family or a friend."

ANOTHER WEEK WENT BY and still nobody got arrested. Most of the FBI and the other out-of-town police packed up and left. Daddy said Raymond told him there would be what he called a "task force" left to keep on investigating but I never saw any of them.

Peggy had a great imagination and always had some new theory about the Barber, but Joyce and I got bored with it all and decided it was time to start playing hospital again. There was no telling how many patients needed to be vaccinated.

"Doctors always have to be on call," Joyce said, "and we have been neglecting our duty."

The next afternoon we played until it almost got too dark under the house to see how to wrap up our last patient in toilet paper. "I'm going home," Joyce said, "we can bury him tomorrow."

After she left I put my syringes in the medicine chest in my doctor's office. Actually, it's not a real medicine chest, just an old cigar box Daddy threw away. The boxes also make good Emergency Rooms where I keep lizards until time to vaccinate them.

As I started to climb the back steps I saw something move along the side of the Little House. I tiptoed over and, sure enough, it was a lizard – a big one. I was determined to catch him and pop him into an Emergency Room so we would have a patient ready to work on when Joyce came tomorrow.

The lizard ran along the foundation bricks and stopped, watching me as I crept closer and closer. I made a grab for him but he was too quick. He scurried across the grass, climbed up the side of the trash barrel and disappeared inside.

I need to tell you that Daddy empties our garbage and trash into a big steel barrel that sits behind the Little House. Mother is always complaining that the City of Moss Point should pick up the garbage like big cities do, but Daddy says they would have to raise taxes to pay the garbage men and he already pays too much taxes. So he gives a guy a dollar a month to come by every once in a while to empty the barrel and haul the garbage away. The man's supposed to come every week, but sometimes he forgets or something and the barrel overflows.

He must have forgotten to come by this week – and last week, too – because trash was overflowing the top of the barrel. But the lizard was in there somewhere and I was determined to catch him. The lid was half off the barrel so I pushed it all the way off. The clatter when it hit the ground would have waked up the dead people in Griffin Cemetery. I was glad our renter had already gone to the shipyard for his night shift.

There was no way the lizard could escape so I took my time pulling stuff out, making sure I didn't miss the little rascal. I was on tiptoe, leaning way over, when I grabbed a handful of something that felt like long silky threads. I pulled it up so I could see it better and, to my puzzlement, saw I was holding long strands of hair. At just that moment, the last rays of the setting sun poked through the leaves of a tree and flickered across my hand and the thin sheaf of hair. In an instant, like turning on a magic switch, the ribbons of hair blazed flaming red.

I was so surprised – maybe stunned is a better word – that my thick brain wouldn't answer the questions that were jostling back and forth in my head. Then, like a light bulb clicking on, I knew. Daddy's words came flooding back. The murdered woman, he had said, "… had pretty red hair and the barber had whacked off a hank on one side."

Totally absorbed in my discovery, I failed to hear the foot-step behind me.

Chapter Twelve

THE AWFUL SMELLING RAG smushed against my face, covering my nose and mouth. A strong, hairy arm reached around me, pinning my arms to my body. I tried to holler but the rag was pressed so tight my cries came out as wimpy moans. Maybe I could hold my breath until I somehow got loose, I thought, but it was no use. I had to breathe. When I did, the stuff on the rag made the inside of my nose and mouth and throat burn like crazy.

I twisted and turned, trying to escape, but the person holding me was strong – really, really strong. I kicked and kicked, as hard and fast as I could – and heard my shoes drumming against the steel trash barrel. The drumming got fainter and fainter, like a brass band marching away down the street. At the end, the drumming – and everything else – faded into darkness.

❧❧

CHAPTER THIRTEEN

WATER. I DESPERATELY WANTED a drink of water. My throat was burning. I was thirsty, so thirsty. Water. Please. Please give me a drink of water.

These were the first thoughts that rose in my slow-moving, mixed-up brain. Then others followed. Where was I? Why can't I move? Why can't I see? Who did this to me?

I heard a car door open, then close. A heavy cover, like a tarpaulin maybe, was thrown back and strong hands lifted me – and dumped me on the ground. I still couldn't move, but now I realized why. I seemed to be rolled up in a thick, scratchy piece of canvas that smelled like tar and dead fish.

The canvas had loosened when I bumped on the ground and I could now see through an edge that was half unfolded. Although I couldn't locate it, the moon was up there some-where, painting everything in silvery light. Outlined against the lighter sky was the dark silhouette of a huge live oak tree. The shape looked familiar. Where had I seen that tree before?

The man – I had decided it must be a man because he was so strong – was putting something in the car. He backed out and closed the door carefully without slamming it. We must be close to houses, I thought, or he wouldn't be moving so quietly. Maybe somebody would hear me if I hollered. I tried to open my mouth to scream – but it wouldn't open. I wasn't gagged, so there must be a piece of tape across my mouth. I decided not to make a sound or try to move. I didn't want that awful rag on my face again.

Bending quickly, the man picked me up and held me snugly under his arm – like you would carry a rolled-up rug. As he turned and started walking, I recognized where we were. He had pulled off onto the little dirt road that led down to Nettie's house.

I also got a good luck at his car, now half-hidden in the shrubbery. Except it wasn't a car, it was an old Ford pickup, one I easily recognized. I should have, because I had seen it every day for months, parked by the side of the Little House.

The man – could it be our renter? – walked briskly down the road toward the pogy plant. I knew that's where he was headed because the smell got stronger and stronger. As we got closer I began to hear the throb and clatter of the machinery. I remember being surprised; I didn't know the plant operated at night. But then, they had a lot of pogies to unload and pulverize.

My brain was working better now, and the pieces of the puzzle were coming together, painting a picture of what had happened. My troubles had begun when I started chasing the lizard. It was then I made an assumption that was horribly,

horribly wrong – the assumption that our renter already had driven off to begin his nightshift at Ingalls. But he must have been running late. He was still in the Little House when I made all that racket around the trash barrel.

He must have been watching me through a window. When he saw me pull out the sheaf of hair, he knew he had to act – and fast.

THE MAN STOPPED AT THE EDGE of the parking lot. I couldn't see his face but he must have been making sure no one was there or at the back of the pogy plant. Adjusting his grip on me, he walked quickly across the lot and into the shadows behind the building. When he shifted me, I wound up looking down at the ground. I saw clearly each iron step and splintery floorboard as he climbed the stairs, rolled back the big door and entered the stuffy heat and pounding noise of the pogy plant.

He was moving toward the pulverizer; the grinding and slashing and crushing noises grew louder and louder. He stopped beside the conveyor belt. An unending stream of small fish rolled past and disappeared into the flashing knives of the giant machine. What is this guy doing? What does he plan to do with me? Why has he stopped at the pulverizer? The questions flew back and forth in my brain.

The answer exploded in a blinding flash of light. My body turned cold as ice. Fear literally paralyzed me. This could not be! God would not let me be murdered like this!

I was so terrified I couldn't breathe normally, plus my nose was full of glop. All I could do was take short half breaths, sucking in the hot, humid air of the plant like a fish pulled out of the water.

The man laid me on the floor beside the conveyor belt. He must have had some shred of kindness because he pulled out a piece of cloth – maybe a handkerchief – and tied it like a blindfold over my eyes. Then he lifted me up and over – toward the conveyor belt.

I knew I'd better pray – and pray hard – so I started the Lord's Prayer. "Our father who art in heaven … our father who art in heaven … our father who art in heaven … ." I couldn't remember what came next! My brain was paralyzed.

The man must have tripped as he turned toward the conveyor belt, because he gave a loud grunt and – dropped me on the floor! If I hadn't been rolled up in that piece of canvas I just know every bone in my body would have broken. I heard another grunt that was almost a scream and he stepped on my leg. Then I got kicked and stepped on again, and again. What was he doing? What was going on?

I tried to roll away so I wouldn't get kicked and stepped on, and found that I could simply unroll myself out of the canvas. Kicking off the last layer, I crawled as fast as I could away from the noise of the pulverizer.

Ouch! I bumped headfirst into something hard and suddenly remembered I was blindfolded. I tried to pull it off but it was tied so tight I was only able to tug up one corner. But that was enough to let me see out of one eye. I scrambled – half crawling, half walking – toward the big door. Behind me I heard two dull thuds and then a sound I will never forget if I live to be a hundred.

The scream began deep in the man's throat and seemed torn out of his very soul. Louder and louder it rose and then, like it was cut off with a knife, the scream ended. The steady rumble of the pulverizer slowed, then stuttered. The electric lights overhead dimmed, flickered bright, dimmed again, then blazed as brightly as ever. The pulverizer picked up speed and returned to its steady rumble.

I never looked back. Stumbling down the iron steps, I ran, not very fast, across the parking lot. My legs were stiff and cramped and I seemed to be running in slow motion. But I had to get away. I didn't know who had screamed. Maybe it was a workman who had tried to save me. In any event, the killer would come after me. He couldn't afford to let me live.

I pushed into the bushes on the far side of the parking lot and stopped. My nose was full of stuff and I was having real trouble breathing. I ripped off the tape that covered my mouth and sucked in a wonderful deep breath of air. Then I cautiously parted the bushes and looked back at the pogy plant.

A man was coming down the iron steps. I squinted, one-eyed, but I couldn't make out his face in the darkness. My breath caught in my throat. It must be the killer. It must be. I had to run. Run and hide. I hesitated a moment, watching to see which way he would go.

The man stopped at the bottom of the steps, bent over and picked up something. Straightening, he placed whatever it was on his head, drew his shoulders back and walked briskly across the parking lot and into the darkness. As the shadows swallowed him, the pale moonlight glinted briefly on the shiny top hat.

CHAPTER FOURTEEN

I COULD HEAR WORKMEN hollering inside the pogy plant. Abruptly, somebody poked his head out the back door and looked quickly around. Then he backed up and rolled the big door shut. It was time for me to go.

Pushing through the bushes, I found the road and started walking toward home. In no time at all, a police car screeched to a stop and a policeman hopped out.

"Are you Pollye Franklin?" he asked.

"Yes, sir," I managed to croak.

"Well, everybody in Jackson County is looking for you. Are you OK? Do I need to take you to the hospital?"

"No, sir. Please, just take me home."

MOTHER WAS THE FIRST ONE to grab me when the policeman lifted me out of the car. Daddy was next and I thought they were going to smother me with hugs and drown me with tears. They probably would have if the odor of dead fish and tar hadn't been so strong.

"Oh, Pollye, my precious little Pollye," Mother kept saying over and over. She would hug me for a moment, then hold me at arm's length and take a deep breath, then hug me again.

On the last hug I lost it. I couldn't help bawling like a baby. They were so wonderful and I loved them so much. The thought of being murdered and never seeing them again was more than I could stand.

Somebody wiped my tears with a handkerchief or something. I blinked and saw it was Dick. He was crying, too, and I lost it again. It was so good to be loved – so good – so blessed good.

AT LAST THE TEARS RAN DRY and, for the first time, I had a chance to look around. I couldn't believe it. The porch, the front steps, and the yard were packed with people – Mr. and Mrs. Armistead and Mr. and Mrs. Khayat and Mrs. Suthoff and Peggy and Joyce and little Mary and Edna and her little brother Eddie and her littler brother Robert and our preacher and two of my teachers and Dr. Ely and a scads of other people I barely knew. Then the whole crowd did something that made goose bumps pop up all over me – everybody there started clapping and cheering and most of the ladies started crying. I think they were glad I was safely home. I know I sure was!

Sheriff Hardy and several policemen were standing off to the side. The Sheriff nodded and smiled when I looked his way. Dr. Ely was the first one to speak.

"Arlis, bring into the front bedroom. I need to make sure she's alright."

The doctor was a gentle man who didn't seem to mind the fish smell at all. After he examined me, he turned to Mother.

"Maud, she's OK. Just some bad bruises in various places and a scraped knee." He turned back to me. "Pollye, is your throat sore?"

"Yes, sir," My voice was still raspy and croaky. "It really burns."

"I thought so." He pulled a little flat stick out of his bag and took another look at my throat.

"Hmmmmm," the doctor murmured. I wondered what that meant – good news or bad news?

Turning to Mother, he said, "Maud, I'll give Charlie Armistead a couple of prescriptions. One is for a throat rinse. I want you to help her gargle with that every three hours until her throat feels better. The other is for a soothing loz-enge – sort of like a cough drop – that she can let dissolve in her mouth. Pollye," he patted me on the shoulder, "you'll feel much better tomorrow."

I hoped so.

Dr. Ely stopped outside my door and I could hear several men talking. In a moment he stepped back into my room.

"Sheriff Hardy needs to talk to you, Pollye. They need to find out what happened as quickly as possible." He nodded to Mother.

"It's OK for her to talk, just not too long or too loud."

SHERIFF HARDY CAME IN WITH Daddy and two of the policemen. I think one of them was the Police Chief. There was only one chair so Mother and Daddy and I sat on the side of my bed. Mother held my hands, giving me a loving squeeze from time to time, and Daddy had a protective arm around my shoulders. Sheriff Hardy nodded at a lady I hadn't noticed before and she quickly sat down in the chair. Her hands trembled slightly as she opened a briefcase and took out a notepad and several pencils.

"Polly," Sheriff Hardy started to say something to Daddy but stopped in confusion. Then he grinned and shook his head. "I think I'd better refer to you as Arlis instead of using your nickname. Miss Ada," he glanced at the lady, "will never be able to figure out which Polly I'm talking to."

"Anyway, this won't take long. But we've got to find out what happened so the Chief and his boys can get busy." He turned to me.

"Pollye, please, mam, tell us what happened to you tonight."

I took a deep breath and told the story from the time I chased the lizard into the trash barrel to the point where the police car stopped to pick me up. My throat hurt more and more and, by the time I finished, I was barely croaking. One of the policemen fumbled in his shirt pocket and pulled out a stick of Juicy Fruit chewing gum.

"Would this help?" he asked and handed it to Mother.

She peeled the paper off and popped the stick of gum in my mouth. I closed my eyes and chewed, then let the juice dribble down my throat. Oh, it felt so good!

"Thank you, sir," I managed to say. This time I didn't sound quite so much like a dying frog.

Sheriff Hardy and the policemen stood up.

"Chief," the Sheriff said, "you and me and the boys got a lot of work to do tonight."

Chapter Fifteen

HEAVY FOOTSTEPS IN THE living room, a lot of heavy footsteps, dragged me awake. I blinked in the bright sunlight flooding my bedroom. I knew where I was, of course – smack dab in the middle of my beautiful four-poster bed – but I couldn't recall how I got there or even what day this was. I tried to focus my thoughts by concentrating on the intricate brass rosette in the center of the grand, full-tester canopy that loomed like a protective roof above me.

I loved my bed. Mother bought it for me at the Old Place in Gautier and told me it had once belonged to a wealthy Creole family in New Orleans. I often wondered – even dreamed – of the young girl who first slept in my bed. I longed to know more about her. Was she beautiful? Was she happy? Did she have friends who played with her – carefully arranging the exquisite lace dresses of their porcelain dolls on the counterpane of my bed? Did she say her nightly prayer in English or in French? I hoped it was in French – that was much more romantic. Some day, I decided, I would learn to say the Lord's Prayer in French.

The voices of the men interrupted my thoughts. I recognized the Sheriff's voice and realized he and the policemen must be telling Daddy and Mother what they had found last night. The Sheriff was talking.

" ... searched the Little House first. The boys found the hank of hair draped over the side of the trash barrel, just where Pollye dropped it. Then we took the Little House apart and ... ," he was interrupted by what sounded like a half-groan, half-sob from Mother.

"Now, don't get upset, Miz Franklin, we were real careful and didn't break a thing. What I meant was that the boys searched every inch, inside and out. They didn't find any more hanks of hair, but they did find this."

What had they found? I hopped out of bed, tiptoed to the door and squinted through the keyhole. At first I couldn't see anything but some guy's backside. Then the backside moved away and I saw what the Sheriff was holding – a large pair of scissors. Very carefully, he placed the scissors in a cellophane bag that somebody's hands were holding. As he did, I had a good look at the blades. They were very long and very sharp.

"He obviously washed and even scrubbed all the blood stains away," Sheriff Hardy explained, "but the doc said the blades are a perfect fit for the death wound on the victim."

"Where did you find them?" Daddy's voice asked.

Another voice answered, apparently one of the policemen. "They was taped underneath the sink in the little kitchen. Hit was a good hidin' place; we almost missed 'em."

"Oh, nooo," Mother groaned. "I can't believe a murderer was living right in our back yard."

"Yes, mam," another voice chimed in. "Y'all were mighty lucky he didn't hurt none of y'all."

There was an awkward silence. They were wondering the same thing I was – has this guy forgotten the killer almost pulverized me?

His mistake apparently dawned on him and he fumbled to explain. "I mean … you know …."

"Shut up, Abner," the Sheriff cut him off in a voice that was both tired and disgusted.

Daddy's voice broke the awkward silence. "You said you went to the pogy plant, too. Find anything there?"

"Yes, sir, we did," the Sheriff answered. "The whole night shift was still standing around the pulverizer when we got there. They were pretty excited and it took a while to quiet 'em down so the foreman could tell us what had happened. Seems everything was going along normally when, all of a sudden, they heard a horrible scream and the pulverizer slowed down like it was chokin' up on something. Then the lights dimmed – the pulverizer is powered by a big electric motor, you know – and the foreman ran to turn off the power at the main switch box. Before he got there, though, the lights came back on, bright as ever, and the pulverizer sped up to its normal operating speed."

The men in our living room were quiet for a moment, sickened by thoughts of what must have happened – the unspeakable horror that slowed the pulverizer and dimmed the lights. I squeezed my eyes tightly shut, trying to will those thoughts out of my own mind. I desperately wanted to forget all that had happened, to hide in some dark room where there were no memories.

At last, one of the policemen spoke quietly. "Tell 'em about the cap, Sheriff."

"Yeah," Sheriff Hardy responded, his voice husky with emotion. "The foreman said he found two things on the floor next to the pulverizer. One was part of a heavy canvas tarp that must have been used to cover a fish box. It's what the killer rolled little Pollye up in." He paused to let that sink in. "And by the way, it stinks to high heaven. Don't know where we're gonna store it."

"What was the other thing the foreman found?" Daddy asked.

"This," the Sheriff answered.

I heard the rustling of a paper bag. The Sheriff was off to the right of the keyhole somewhere and I couldn't see what he was pulling from the sack. When he handed it across to Daddy, though, I saw it clearly. A dirty, black-and-white striped work cap like railroad engineers wore. The renter always had it own when I saw him going to work.

"If you look on the sweat band," the Sheriff said, "you'll see a name printed there in ink. Pretty faded, but look closely. You'll see it."

Daddy held the cap in the light and slowly read, "H. Spragins." He turned to Mother. "That's the renter's name, isn't it Maud?"

"Yes," Mother answered, almost whispering. "He always just signed his rent checks 'H. Spragins.'" She thought for a moment. "He also wrote his name that way on the Rent Contract he signed. I can get it if you need to see it, Sheriff."

"No, mam," Sheriff Hardy replied. "I may need it later, but not now."

"Tell 'em what the Rogers boy saw, Sheriff," one of the policeman said.

"Yep," Sheriff Hardy answered, "*that* is a real puzzler. The boy – I forget what his given name is – was the first workman to get to the pulverizer. Said when he rounded the corner of the machine he saw a man – or somebody – going down those iron steps at the back. Actually, all he saw was the back of the person's head. It was dark and he couldn't tell if it was a man or a woman, black or white. Said he stopped to look at the cap and the tarp lying on the floor, and by the time he got to the back door and looked out, there was nobody in sight."

I had a sudden sinking spell. I was hoping that nobody had seen Daniel at the scene. I knew, just knew, that Sheriff Hardy was going to ask me about that. What would my answer be?

"Miz Franklin," the Sheriff said, "I need to talk to little Pollye again. Need to ask her about several things we didn't know when we talked to her last night."

"She's still asleep, Sheriff, but I'll get her up and dressed so you can talk to her. In the meantime, y'all go back to the kitchen. I asked Lena to have a pot of coffee ready when you came in. There may be some biscuits left, too, if Arlis and Dick haven't eaten them all."

There was a shuffling of feet in the living room, then footsteps that faded down the hall. I made a beeline for the bed. When Mother quietly opened the door and came in, I was covered up, apparently sound asleep.

I SNEEZED. TWICE. I COULDN'T help it. Mother was pounding me all over with one of her powder puffs. Clouds of pink powder drifted over the room.

"This will help," she said, "but you still smell a little fishy."

"How is that possible?" I wailed. "You scrubbed most of my skin off last night in the bath tub."

She smiled and gave me a wonderful hug. "I don't mind how you smell, but I want you to be your best when you talk to Sheriff Hardy."

My smile went away. I dreaded that talk. I didn't want him to ask me about anybody I might have seen at the pogy plant. The more I thought about it, the more convinced I became that I should never tell the Sheriff – or anyone – about Daniel and what he did.

What word had Mother used once to describe Daniel? I thought hard and it came to me. "Fragile." That was the word she had used. I didn't know what it meant, so I had looked it up in the big dictionary on the hall table. The definition was scary: "… an object easily broken … a vulnerable person … a personality easily destroyed."

Yes, "fragile" was a perfect description of Daniel. In many ways, he was as delicate – and as vulnerable – as his little feathered friends. Being interrogated by intimidating police-men, grilled about killing a man, handcuffed, locked in a jail cell, put on trial in a courtroom full of strangers – all of that would destroy a personality as fragile as his.

I made my decision. I would never, ever, tell anyone about Daniel and how he saved my life. Not even my own parents.

CHAPTER SIXTEEN

ONCE AGAIN, MOTHER, DADDY and I sat on the side of my bed. This time there were no policemen, just Sheriff Hardy. He sat in the chair across from us and fiddled with the file of papers in his lap. He seemed nervous, perhaps not wanting to ask the questions he had to ask me. He cleared his throat and looked up at me.

"Miss Pollye, this case is just about wrapped up. The mystery of the Midnight Barber is a mystery no longer. We know *who* the barber was and I'm working on a theory that could explain the "*why*" part of it – you know, the motive that made him do it. There's one part of the story, however, that puzzles me."

I cringed inside. He was about to ask the question.

"One of the witnesses, a young fellow that works at the pogy plant, told us he was the first one to reach the pulverizer after all the commotion. He said that when he came around the corner of the machine, he saw a person going down the iron stairs at the back of the plant."

Sheriff Hardy looked down at the file and frowned. I almost smiled – the wrinkles on his forehead looked like the rows in Daddy's garden.

"Well, actually," the Sheriff continued, "the boy only saw the back of that person's head. He can't tell us whether it was a man or woman, or even if it was a white person."

"Is he sure he saw a person?" Daddy asked.

"Pretty sure, but you know he must have been mighty excited – and there was no light outside the building. Could have been his imagination."

Sheriff Hardy riffled through the papers in the file, studied one with pencil notes on it, shook his head and closed the file.

"What I don't understand, though, is why Spragins, even if he stumbled and fell onto the conveyor belt, let himself be dragged into the pulverizer. Why didn't he, or why couldn't he get off the belt?"

He turned to me. "Miss Pollye, you told us the man seemed to stumble and then he dropped you onto the floor."

I didn't know whether that was a question but I answered, "Yes, sir."

"And then you said you were kicked and stepped on, several times."

"Yes, sir, I was. That was when I rolled out of the canvas, or whatever it was, and crawled away."

The Sheriff scratched his chin thoughtfully. "Did you, at any time, see another man in the pogy plant?"

There was no doubt about this one. It was a question – *the* question.

"No, sir, I did not see anyone, man or woman, in the pogy plant." I hesitated, then added, "In fact, I never actually saw Mr. Spragins. All I saw of him was his hands when he tied the blindfold on me."

"Did you hear any words, curse words, threats or anything like that?" The Sheriff was persistent.

"No, sir. The only thing I heard at any time was that awful scream." I shivered, then added, "And I can't get that out of my mind."

Mother squeezed my hand tightly and started to say something. Daddy spoke first.

"Raymond, I've been thinking. When Spragins stumbled and fell, he could have hit his head and knocked himself half out. That would account for why he didn't, or couldn't, manage to get off the conveyor belt before it dumped him in."

Sheriff Hardy nodded, slowly at first, then with more conviction. "Yep, that would account for it." He paused and grinned broadly. "Polly," he used Daddy's nickname, "I believe you have solved the puzzle!"

He slapped the file closed and stood up. I couldn't help but notice that he never once looked me straight in the eye. He had found a logical explanation for the inconsistencies and he didn't want me – by words or facial expression – to create any doubt about his neat conclusion.

"Miz Franklin," he said to Mother, "I want to thank you, all of you, for your cooperation and help in this case. It was tough for all of us and I want you to know I personally appreciate what you've done. And Polly," he slapped Daddy on the shoulder, "I couldn't have solved it without you!"

Daddy beamed. Mother dabbed at a tear wandering down her cheek.

"And Miss Pollye," the Sheriff leaned down and this time he looked me straight in the eye, "we for sure could never have solved the case without you. You are a brave little lady – and a smart one. You know, the next time I get a tough case, I just may call on you to help us solve it!"

He straightened and put on his hat. "And now, folks, I'm going back to the office and dictate my final report. Then I'm gonna put this file," he waggled it in his hand, "in the "Case Closed" drawer and throw away the key!"

I LET OUT A HUGE SIGH of relief when the front door closed behind him. It was over and I had not told any lies. Every word I had said was true: I never saw any other person, or heard any other person, *inside* the pogy plant. And thank goodness, the Sheriff never asked me if I saw anybody *outside* the building!

❧❧

CHAPTER SEVENTEEN

A WEEK WENT BY, THEN another, and people pretty much stopped asking me questions about what the *Pascagoula Chronicle* called my "hairbreadth escape." I sure hadn't forgotten about it though, and one evening when Daddy, Mother and I were eating supper – Dick had a date and was off somewhere with his crowd – I asked Daddy if he ever found out what the Sheriff's theory was, the one about the Barber's motive. He finished chewing a mouthful of butterbeans and laid down his fork.

"Yep, he did tell me, and it's a lollapalooza. It sounds plausible, though, and I believe Raymond got it right."

"Well, tell us about it!" Mother said, her eyes bright with interest.

"OK, here's Raymond's theory. He told me he'd found out during the investigation that Spragins and the woman he killed … "

81

"Leona Murphy," Mother interrupted him. "Her name was Leona Murphy."

"That's right," Daddy said, sounding a little tired. "Anyway, she and Spragins had been dating for over a year and he wanted to get married. But Leona had her eye on somebody with more money than Spragins, one of the executives who was head of the division she worked in. Well, one thing led to another until one night Spragins caught them together in the office. That, Raymond said, was the beginning of the end for Leona."

Mother quickly cupped her hands over my ears and frowned at Daddy.

"Now, don't get excited," Daddy said, "I'm not going to say anything that Polly shouldn't hear. Anyway," he continued, "Raymond believes that Spragins decided then and there to kill Leona, but he had to do it in a way that he wouldn't get caught."

Daddy took a sip from his ice tea glass.

"According to Raymond's theory," he continued, "Spragins knew he couldn't up and kill Leona right away. He'd be the number one suspect for sure. So, he decided to create a 'red herring,' as Raymond called it. He would begin cutting various women's hair, women who didn't know him, and then after ten or twelve of these, he would cut Leona's hair and kill her at the same time. That way, Raymond said, suspicion wouldn't be directed immediately on Spragins. The police would simply think the Barber was some nut who had the misfortune to kill one of his victims."

Mother nodded slowly. "That sounds right to me," she said. "You know, I never thought Raymond was smart enough to figure out something like that."

"Humph!" Daddy said and took another swallow of ice tea.

"But what about Daniel?" Mother asked. "How did he fit in?"

"Well, Raymond believes that Spragins must have had a heart attack – or almost had one – when he heard that Daniel had been arrested as a suspect in the Barber case. If he killed Leona while Daniel was in jail, he'd be right back in the boat he started out in. He'd be suspect number one in the murder case."

"So Spragins must have been very, very happy when he read that Daniel had been released from jail," Mother said. She had really gotten interested in Raymond's theory. "And Spragins didn't know that Daniel and Nettie were locked in the jail every night. That was never in the paper."

"Yep," Daddy said. "Raymond thinks that when Spragins heard the judge had released Daniel from jail, he realized he had to act quickly if he was going to kill Leona. If the police found more evidence against Daniel and locked him up again, Spragins would lose the opportunity."

Daddy picked up his fork and he and Mother finished supper in silence. I toyed with the butterbeans on my plate, no longer hungry. I couldn't get that awful night out of my thoughts. I went over and over each detail. Had I missed something? Was there any reason to doubt Sheriff Hardy's conclusions about the identity of the Barber or about the motive that drove Spragins to murder that poor lady? I finally decided the Sheriff had gotten it right. The entire tragedy, a terrible series of events that brought weeks of fear and mistrust and terror to so many people, must have unfolded pretty much like the Sheriff said.

Daddy gave his plate a final swab with a piece of cornbread, popped it in his mouth and pushed back from the table. He looked over at me.

"You're mighty quiet, Pollye. Do you have any other questions I could answer for you?"

Startled, I looked up at him. "No, sir. My questions have all been answered."

ଓଓ

CHAPTER EIGHTEEN

IN THE WEEKS THAT FOLLOWED, people gradually lost interest in the case of the Midnight Barber. Too many calamities and other exciting things were happening every day in the war. Most of the boys over eighteen were in service or waiting to be called up. And several times a month the *Pascagoula Chronicle* carried a sad story about some boy from Moss Point or Pascagoula being wounded or killed or "missing in action."

Dick couldn't stand being left out and had gotten a part-time job at a boatyard that was building landing craft out of plywood. Plywood! Can you imagine? Anyway, Dick's job was to crawl under the boats and callk (I'm not sure how you spell it) the seams with tar. Sometimes the hot tar would drip on his clothes or even on his skin. When I asked him if it hurt, he looked at me like I was twirp, and using his biggest grown-up voice said, "Nahhh, it's just part of my job!"

He did need help getting the tar off his skin, however, so Mother experimented with everything from gasoline to soap. Finally, she found that nail polish remover worked best. Nail polish remover! I couldn't help it. I had to laugh.

HALF WAY THROUGH THE SCHOOL year following my "hairbreadth escape," something really sad happened. Mother told us at supper one evening that Nettie had suffered a heart attack and was in the hospital. There was no one to look after Daniel or to cook his meals, so Mother organized her WSCS Circle and they took turns delivering food to Nettie's house.

After a couple of weeks, Nettie got better and the doctors released her from the hospital. But it was clear, Mother said, that she would never be able to work again. There was only one thing they could do. Nettie and Daniel would have to move to Hattiesburg to live with her younger sister.

I went with Mother the morning she carried Nettie and Daniel to the bus station. When we drove up to their little house they were waiting patiently on the front porch, Nettie sitting on an upended old suitcase. Mother got out and she and Daniel helped Nettie into our car. They had only the one suitcase. When Daniel seemed unsure what to do with it, I showed him how to open the trunk of the car and helped him lay the suitcase in it. His belongings – I suppose it was everything he owned – were rolled up and tied tightly in an old quilt.

Mother and I got in the car and Daniel, after a little hesitation, started to get in behind Nettie. He stopped abruptly with one foot on the running board, then hopped quickly up the steps and disappeared into the house. I wondered why they hadn't locked the door, but then – what was there to steal? In a moment he reappeared, wearing the shiny top hat. He gave us a big grin, carefully removed the hat, and clambered into the car.

Mother bought each of them a one-way ticket to Hattiesburg and then gave Nettie five ten-dollar bills. "Oh, no, Miz Franklin," Nettie protested, "you done been way too good to us already."

"Take the money, Nettie, you and Daniel are going to need it."

Nettie burst out crying and hugged Mother and reached out to drag me into the huddle. "We ain't got nothin' to give you and little Pollye, Miz Franklin. Not nothin' atall."

Daniel looked perplexed, then brightened and reached into his shirt pocket. He fished out a whole, unbroken pecan half that he held out to me, grinning and nodding his head. I took it and gave him the biggest hug I've ever given anybody in my life. Then I got back in the car as fast as I could. I didn't want anybody to see the tears.

Mother and I sat for a moment in the car, waiting until they disappeared into the bus station. That was the last time I would ever see Dapper Dan and Nettie.

THAT WAS A HARD, COLD WINTER, even in South Mississippi. I don't know whether the temperature had any-thing to do with what happened, but about two months after we put Nettie and Daniel on the bus, Mother received a letter, written in pencil on smudged tablet paper. It was from Nettie's sister. A few days before, Nettie had suffered a massive heart attack. She was dead before a doctor could reach her.

Mother wiped away our tears and asked a question neither of us could answer. "What will become of Daniel?"

We found the answer three days later when another envelope arrived, also postmarked Hattiesburg. There was no letter in this one, only a folded newspaper clipping. I scotch taped the clipping to this page of my story.

> "About 3:00 p.m. yesterday an unidentified white man darted in front of a large truck at the busy intersection of Hardy Street and W. Pine Street in downtown Hattiesburg. The driver valiantly attempted to avoid the man but was unsuccessful.
>
> Police reported there was no identification on the body but that the man apparently was going to a costume party, being dressed in a black frock coat and wearing a black silk opera hat. The man and the hat were crushed by the wheels of the truck."

Chapter Nineteen

ALMOST A DECADE HAS PASSED since my encounter with the Midnight Barber. Today, people rarely mention him or the terror he created – or even his bizarre death. I suspect that most folks simply have forgotten him. I will never forget him – but then I have a very special reason to remember.

My senior year at good ole Moss Point High School has been exciting and chock full of fun – one of the happiest times of my life. In fact, I sometimes need to pinch myself to escape my magical dream world and return to the realities of homework, study and looming exams.

MOTHER PROVIDED A TEMPORARY return to reality one Saturday morning in the early spring. Wearing her gardening clothes and carrying a trowel, she aroused me from a warm, lazy half-nap on the front screen porch.

"Up, up, Pollye, and put on some old clothes and your tennis shoes. We're off to dig up some daffodil bulbs. Your Daddy is already in the car and we need your help!"

WHEN DADDY SLOWED AND turned into a narrow lane, I was daydreaming, lazily tracing the steps of a new dance Joyce Nelson was teaching us, one she had learned at Ole Miss. My daydreams quickly evaporated as we bumped over ruts and potholes and swished through weeds and tall grass. We had traveled some distance before I realized where we were – the driveway leading to the little house where Nettie and Daniel once lived. When I looked questioningly at Mother, she explained our trip.

"Nettie or someone planted several big beds of daffodil bulbs. I remember how beautiful they were – just a mass of color when they bloomed. Nobody's lived here since Nettie left, but the bulbs should still be here – unless somebody else has dug them up."

She gave an audible sigh of relief when Daddy bumped to a stop in front of the little house. "They're still here, thank goodness. But just look at that poor old house!"

We all stared at what remained of the once neat little house. Pieces of the tin roof had blown away – probably during one of the hurricanes that visit the Coast almost every year – and the bare rafters looked like the rib bones of a skeleton. Only shards of broken glass remained in the windows, and the front porch had an interesting tilt to one side. Not much else was visible; tall bushes and weeds – even small trees – grew almost to the eaves all around the walls.

"Well, let's get to work!" Daddy's voice had the authoritative tone of a drill sergeant. He began dragging trowels, hoes, swing blades and croker sacks from the trunk. I sighed and accepted the trowel he thrust toward me.

The daffodils had finished blooming last week, Mother said, and the once golden petals now drooped in brown, straggly strings. They were barely visible, however, beneath the jungle of weeds and grass that covered the beds. Daddy attacked first, chopping out the overgrowth and raking it away from the daffodils. Mother came next. She dropped to her knees and, using a trowel, carefully dug around a clump of bulbs.

"Be careful with the trowel, Pollye. Try not to cut the bulbs."

I sank to my knees beside her and tested the dirt with my trowel. It was soft and moist and teeming with life – red worms, juicy grubs, scurrying ants, tiny, darting spiders – all living in the tangled, thread-like roots of grass and weeds. The rich warm smell of the earth was intoxicating. I inhaled deeply, relishing the rare exhilaration of deeply felt pleasure.

"Thank you, Lord," my silent prayer of gratitude was spontaneous. "Thank you for letting me be a small part of your great universe."

"THESE SHOULD HAVE BEEN dug up every second year and separated," Mother announced in an exasperated voice. "Just look at that." She tugged at a large tangled mass of bulbs and roots.

"They'll have to be separated, but we can do that at home. Hold the sack open, Pollye, this is heavy!"

We worked steadily for a while and our sack of bulbs grew heavier. Mother paused and, using the back of her wrist, brushed an errant lock of hair out of her eyes. Looking around at the house and yard, she slowly shook her head.

"I'm so glad Nettie is not around to see how run down this place is. She worked so hard to keep it clean and neat."

Her comment started me thinking about Nettie and Daniel and the birds. A memory, long buried and forgotten, came bubbling up in my brain. Nettie had once told Mother that Daniel had built a tree house – that he hid there when he was afraid or wanted to be alone. I wondered if the tree house still existed. Had it rotted away? Where was it?

"Mother, I'm going to walk around for a few minutes. But I'll come back and help you finish."

She nodded and continued digging.

"Watch out for snakes!" Daddy warned.

ONCE I NAVIGATED THE VINES and briars covering the back yard, the walking was much easier in the shade of the giant live oak trees. The faint outline of a path led me deeper into the woods until, abruptly, I found the way blocked by a huge fallen limb. Briars and tall weeds had sprung up around it, creating a formidable roadblock. I had no desire to climb over it, through it, or under it, so I turned to go back. As I did, I saw the tree house, weathered a dull gray and wedged between low hanging limbs of an ancient live oak. Had I not been carefully searching each of the trees, I might never have noticed it.

Stepping carefully, I pushed through the undergrowth to the base of the tree. Daniel had nailed short cross pieces of wood to form a rough ladder, but these were too rotten to trust. Undaunted, I considered other ways to climb to the tree house. I was determined to look inside.

Fortunately, the tree trunk was adorned with nobs and bumps of all sizes, affording adequate handholds and toeholds for an adventurous climber. And the floor of the tree house was no higher than a basketball goal. So, up I went.

Daniel had climbed into his tree house through a sort of trap door in the floor. Cautiously, I poked my head up through the opening. As my eyes adjusted to the shadowy interior, I quickly saw that it was empty – no boxes or broken chairs or anything of value. I was disappointed. And then I noticed the floor was littered with objects that were indistinct in the dusty half-light. I squinted, shielding my eyes from a beam of sunlight pouring through a small opening.

Maybe I was weary from digging daffodil bulbs or from climbing the tree or from struggling through briars and vines, but for some reason my brain refused to acknowledge what I was looking at – strands and coils of human hair!

When finally I understood – and comprehended the enormity of what I had discovered – I almost lost my grip on one of the limbs supporting me. In fact, I was afraid for a moment that I might faint.

I inhaled deeply a couple of times and took a long, hard look at the contents of the tree house. Laid out in neat rows across the floor were strands and whole hanks of hair – ebony hair, blond hair, auburn hair. There were long strands and short ones, curly strands and straight ones.

I looked around more closely – and did a double take. Almost at my fingertips was a large pair of very rusty scissors. They lay on a fragment of moldy, rotting black cloth that appeared to have eyeholes cut in it. I didn't touch the scissors or the mask – or the hair.

Perhaps unconsciously, I had known all along. Now, the truth blazed indelibly before me. Daniel had indeed been the Midnight Barber!

But why? Why had he exerted so much energy and invested so much time in collecting these ridiculous clumps of human hair. More important, why had he assumed such dangerous risks – risks that easily could have culminated in his death?

Impatient blasts from our car's horn told me that Daddy was ready to go home. I hastily scrambled down from the tree house and pushed through the undergrowth to the path. Catching my breath, I considered the question that arose as soon as I realized what lay in the tree house: should I tell the police what I had found? Or for that matter, should I tell my parents?

I tried to focus on the realities of the situation. What good would be accomplished by telling? Daniel, after all, had been dead for almost a decade. The saga of the Midnight Barber was remembered by only a few, and was almost never discussed. My discovery would open long-healed wounds among the women who were victimized. To most everyone else the revelation would be no more than a curiosity. And for me, in some way I still can't explain, I would be violating an unspoken trust.

I made a decision. The secret would belong to me – and to Daniel's little friends.

Before leaving, I paused and looked back one last time at the tree house. At that moment a tiny bird, it looked like a wren, fluttered out of a small opening and sailed through the sun-dappled shade beneath the live oaks. As it flew by me, it passed through a patch of bright sunlight. Trailing from its beak was a long golden strand of hair.

As I watched the little wren disappear into the foliage, an epiphany welled up within me like the bright dawning of a new day. I finally – at last – understood the meaning of it all – the "why" that had motivated Daniel.

I laughed. I *had* to laugh – laugh at the sheer audacity of Daniel's mission – and marvel at his success. For there in the little tree house, available to all, was his legacy – ample material for generations of his little friends to use in building their nests.